P9-CDY-419

254

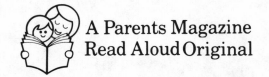

A Parents Magazine
Read Aloud Original

THE PEACE AND QUIET DINER

Story by Gregory Maguire
Pictures by David Perry

PARENTS MAGAZINE PRESS · NEW YORK

Library of Congress Cataloging-in-Publication Data

Maguire, Gregory
The peace and quiet diner / by Gregory Maguire; pictures
by David Perry.
   p. cm.
Summary: Lester worries that his life is not adventurous
enough for his visiting Auntie June, but the diner where
they meet offers plenty of activity after all.
ISBN 0-8193-1176-6
[1. Animals—Fiction.   2. Stories in rhyme.]
I. Perry, David, ill.   II. Title.
PZ8.3.M273Pe   1988
[E]—dc19   87-36865
                                               CIP

Text copyright © 1988 by Gregory Maguire.   AC
Illustrations copyright © 1988 by David Perry.
All rights reserved.
Printed in the United States of America.
10   9   8   7   6   5   4   3   2   1

For Maureen Vecchione—G.M.
To Sue and Nicholas
with special thanks to
Mary Faulconer—D.P.

Lester got a letter
From his Auntie June.
She said she'd come to visit
That very afternoon.
That was very soon.

Lester knew his Auntie well.
She was full of bounce.
She always said, "Don't bore me!
Adventure is what counts!
In very large amounts!"

Lester had a photo
Of Auntie on the Nile.
She was playing tug-of-war
With a crocodile.
She had the larger smile.

Lester had a worry.
Auntie might be bored.
So he called up Morris.
"Help me, friend!" he roared.

Morris said to Lester,
"Don't have a single care.
We'll go out to eat.
Your aunt can meet us there."

The friends met at a diner.
Morris said, "What's wrong?"
Lester said, "My Auntie June
Soon will come along!"

"Auntie loves adventure!
She is not like us!
My life is very simple,
But Auntie loves a fuss!"

The waiter took their order,
Soup and eggs and cheese.
Lester dropped his napkin.
He said, "Excuse me, please."

When he went to find it
Down upon the floor
Morris saw some lions
Enter with a roar!

Lester got his sweater
Caught upon the chair.
Morris didn't notice.
All he did was stare.

Morris looked around him.
The place was getting busy.
So *many* folks arriving!
It almost made him dizzy.
In came seven monkeys
Swinging on the lights.
They were dressed in capes
And fancy sequinned tights.

Then a cat came selling
Raffle tickets, cheap.
"First prize is a trip," she said,
"On the ocean deep!"

Morris had some money,
So he ordered two.
"One for me," he said,
"And Lester, one for you."
The cat went springing off
When a dog began to bark.
Morris saw it all.
Lester just saw dark.

Morris said to Lester,
"This diner is a find!"
Lester didn't listen.
He just looked out the blind.

"Nothing ever happens.
I'm sure that Auntie June
Will find it very boring.
She'll be arriving soon."

Morris watched a rhino
with a feathered hat
Start to sing an opera.
(She sang a little flat.)
The monkeys did athletics.
The lions roared for more.
The rhino did a little dance
That almost broke the floor.

Lester said, "She's coming!"
Said Morris, "Don't despair!
If you'd only keep your eyes peeled
you wouldn't even care—
There's adventure everywhere!"

Auntie June was floating
In her private parachute.
She landed by the diner
In her best safari suit.

The minute that she entered
Everyone began to eat.
"Lester *darling*!" cried his Auntie.
"What a *boring* place to meet!"

Lester only whimpered.
Morris said, "Not so!
This place is fairly hopping!"
Auntie June said, "Oh?"

Just then the cat announced
It was time to have the draw.
She pulled the winning ticket
And she held it in her paw.
"The number is," she read aloud,
"Four hundred forty nine."
Everybody checked, and then
Lester cried, "That's mine!"

"A week's vacation sailing
Upon the deep blue sea!"
The cat shook hands with Lester.
Lester said, "For me?"

He stood up on the table.
He said, "This afternoon
I want to give my prize
to my lovely Auntie June!"

TOMATO JUICE 50¢ | PLEASE PAY WHEN SERVED | HOT CHOCOLATE 75¢ | TEA 50¢

Auntie danced with pleasure.
Auntie was delighted.
She ran off to pack her trunk,
She was that excited.

Lester sat and smiled.
He said, "I must agree.
Adventure's all around you.
You only have to see!"

About the Author

Gregory Maguire has had adventure in his time: He's been charged by a bull elephant in Africa, has crossed a swollen river by canoe in Central America, and has driven on expressways during rush hour. But he is nonetheless very fond of peace and quiet, wherever it can be found.

Mr. Maguire is the author of fantasy and science fiction novels for children and teenagers, and is a favorite speaker at schools across the United States. He lives in Massachusetts.

About the Artist

David Perry is very fond of both animals and diners. But although he enjoyed drawing the *Peace and Quiet Diner,* he wouldn't want to eat at a place like that. "Those animals would be too noisy, even for me," he says.

Mr. Perry's animals first surfaced in 1973; they have since appeared in numerous books and magazines. He is an award-winning designer/ illustrator who, with his wife and young son, splits his time between New York and a farm in Pennsylvania.